PUT THAT LIGHT OUT!

by Jack Wood

Illustrations by Tim Sell

WITHDRAWN FROM STOCK

W
FRANKLIN WATTS
LONDON • SYDNEY

This edition 2005
First published in 2000 by Franklin Watts
96 Leonard Street, London EC2A 4XD

Text © Jack Wood 2000
Illustrations © Tim Sell 2000

The right of Jack Wood to be identified as
the Author of this Work has been asserted by
him in accordance with the Copyright, Designs
and Patents Act, 1988

Editor: Lesley Bilton
Designer: Jason Anscomb
Consultant: Anita M. Ballin, Head of Education,
Imperial War Museum

A CIP catalogue record for this book
is available from the British Library

ISBN 0 7496 6409 6

Dewey Classification 942.084
Printed in Great Britain

PUT THAT LIGHT OUT!

by Jack Wood

Illustrations by Tim Sell

TALES OF THE SECOND WORLD WAR

UNTIL YOUR EYES
GET USED TO
THE DARKNESS
TAKE IT EASY

LOOK OUT IN THE BLACKOUT

Chapter 1
In the Dark

"That's your third accident this month," said Joanie, winding a bandage round Dad's leg. "What happened *this* time?"

Dad groaned. "I fell into a bomb crater. A bike with no lights on ran straight into me!"

"You should have got used to the blackout by now," said Ma, shutting the First Aid tin.

"I'll never get used to it," snorted Dad.* "No street lights! Cars with masked headlamps! Bikes that –"

BANG! The door crashed open and Lenny staggered into the room, clutching a handkerchief to his face. With a hollow cry, he collapsed into a chair.

"Be quiet, or you'll wake your Gran," said Ma, nodding at the sleeping figure in the corner of the room.

"Don't care," howled Lenny. Blood trickled down his face and splashed on the carpet.

"Don't Care was made to care," said Ma, opening the First Aid tin again.

"It's a good job I've been to bandaging class." Joanie peered closely at Lenny's head. "What have *you* fallen into?"

"I walked into a lamp post."

* *Find out more about the blackout on page 60*

"They're alright in Alma Road," piped up Heather. She was sitting on the floor, practising her bandaging on the dog's tail. "Their lamp posts have been painted white, so they show up in the dark."

"They should do the same here in Balaclava Terrace," said Ma.

Joanie shook the iodine bottle vigorously and removed the stopper. "It's too expensive."

"Expensive, huh?" said Lenny, exchanging a look with Dad.

There was a stirring noise from the armchair near the fire. Gran opened one eye.

"There's a shortage of white paint," said Joanie, as she poured some of the iodine on to a pad of cotton wool, and pressed it to Lenny's forehead. "This won't hurt."

"Owwee!" Lenny leapt up with a howl of agony, and tripped over his younger brother, Roy, who'd been sitting quietly on the floor sorting out his cigarette cards.

Roy fell backwards with a thump and kicked the dog.

The dog bit Dad on his injured leg.

"Aaaargh!" Dad screamed, and dropped the beer bottle he was clutching.

"This can't go on," said Ma, snapping shut the First Aid tin. "We've no bandages left. Roy, pay attention! You're supposed to have some brains. I'm making you responsible for seeing that this family has no more accidents."

"But Ma, how am I –"

"You've got to find a way of making Dad stand out in the dark."

Heather sniggered.

"And you can help him, Heather."

The two youngest members of the Pitt family looked at each other.

Then they looked at their father.

Dad wore his usual dirty grey trousers, with his dirty grey vest and his dirty grey cap. His face was a dirty grey colour.

How could they make Dad more visible?

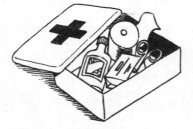

Chapter 2
The Paint Arrives

It wasn't an easy task. Roy sat and brooded about it for most of the next day. Why was it always *him* who had to get the family out of trouble?

"What on earth can I do?" he asked the framed photograph over the mantelpiece.

The whiskered face of Great-Uncle Porker Pitt, an army cook, scowled back at him.

According to Dad, Great-Uncle Porker had died a hero's death during the Siege of Mafeking in 1899 (he'd met a horrible end while searching for rations). Dad was a bit hazy about the details, but it had something to do with a pig.

Roy wondered how he could add to the family glory. Could he invent some kind of clothing that would glow in the dark? That would help the War Effort. The Prime Minister might even give him a medal. He could imagine the scene . . .

The crowded room rang with loud applause.

"And finally, for saving the lives of hundreds of British citizens with his invention of the Pitt Luminous Trousers, this young man is given the highest honour I can award."

"It's nothing, Mr Churchill, why I was only –"

"Stop talking to yourself, Roy." Lenny's head appeared through the open window. "Go and unlock the back door. I've got some stuff here that I don't want Mrs Moan to see."

Roy scrambled to his feet obediently and headed for the kitchen. Mrs Moan was their nosey next-door neighbour. Her real name was Mrs Moon, but she moaned so much that everyone called her Mrs Moan.

He ran into the kitchen, opened the door, and stood aside as Lenny staggered past him carrying two large tins.

"What's in them?" Roy asked.

Lenny looked from side to side. "White paint," he said in a low voice. "I managed to get some."

Roy knew better than to ask how.

"Good lad," said Gran, coming in through the open door carrying a bowl of eggs. "They should fetch a bit of money. Hide them somewhere. Not in the house."

"Sorry, Gran." Heather stumbled into the kitchen clutching a couple of chicken feathers. "She was too quick for me."

With a determined grunt, Gran rolled up her sleeves. "Lenny, I need your help. The white hen's stopped laying, so it's the cooking pot for her! There'll be chicken for dinner tomorrow." Smacking her lips, she stomped back into the garden.

"Here, you two. Hide these somewhere. Not in the house." Thrusting the tins at Roy, Lenny rushed out of the door after Gran.

Roy and Heather looked at each other thoughtfully.

"Mrs Grubb's gone to see her sister up north. I heard her tell Ma that she'd be away for at least TWO WEEKS." Heather raised her voice to a shout. She had to yell because the squawking noises coming from the garden were deafening. "YOU CAN GET INTO MRS GRUBB'S HOUSE, CAN'T YOU?"

"YES. THROUGH THAT HOLE IN OUR ATTIC." Roy looked troubled. "I THINK MRS GRUBB MIGHT BE ANNOYED IF WE HID THESE TINS UP THERE."

There was a last, long, agonised squawk from the garden. Then silence.

"Would you rather annoy Gran?" asked Heather.

Chapter 3
The Warden's Visit

"Don't wriggle about so much Joanie. I can't get these rollers in straight." Ma's mouth was full of hairgrips.

"I bet there's an air raid tonight before you finish my perm," said Joanie, trying not to move her head.

"Depends on the weather." Dad strolled over to the window. "If this fog hangs about, the Jerry bombers won't come." He pulled open the curtain.

"PUT THAT LIGHT OUT, NUMBER 46! DO YOU WANT THE GERMANS TO BLOW YOU ALL TO KINGDOM COME?" A loud voice thundered from the street outside.

"Blimey, it's the Great Dictator," said Dad, closing the curtain. "I can't so much as look at the weather now, without him ordering me about."

The door flew open and Mr Marsh, their local Air-Raid Precautions Warden, charged into the room like an enraged rhinoceros.

"WHAT DO YOU THINK YOU'RE DOING?" Warden Boggy Marsh was a large red-faced man with a *very* loud voice.

"I only lifted up the curtain for a couple of seconds," blustered Dad.

"That's long enough. Enemy bombers could see that light from five thousand feet." The warden strode over to the window and tugged at the blackout curtains. "These aren't long enough. You can see light at the bottom."

"Only if you get down on your knees in the road and peer up. Do you think the German Air Force is going to invade Balaclava Terrace by tunnel?" asked Dad.

"You Pitts have the worst blackout in my district." The veins in the warden's neck swelled. "You're unpatriotic!"

"Unpatriotic!" cried Dad, with bulging eyes. He waved his hand at the photograph of Great-Uncle Porker. "We Pitts have died for our country." He paused and glared round the room. "Tell you what – I'll paint the entire house black. Will that keep you quiet? Black walls, black windows, black door!"

Ma looked unhappy. "I don't –"

"That reminds me," Boggy butted in, shooting a sharp glance at Lenny. "Does anyone know anything about two large tins of white paint?"

Lenny didn't look up from the government leaflet he was reading. It was called *How to Decontaminate People who have been Exposed to Poisonous Gases*, and Lenny seemed to be deeply interested in the subject.

"They disappeared from Mr Harbottle's shop last night," continued the warden, "and the burglar left a ladder leaning –"

"It must be time for the news," said Roy quickly, turning on the wireless. A cheerful voice invaded the room.

"This is the Radio Doctor. How are you today? How are your bowels? It is your duty to help Britain's War Effort by keeping healthy. And healthy bowels will –"

Dad gave a howl of rage, dived at the wireless and turned it off. "Do this! Do that! Is there no peace?" He strode out of the room and slammed the door behind him. The picture of Great-Uncle Porker fell off the wall, and the glass shattered on the floor.

At the same moment, the air-raid siren shrieked. WAAAAAAAAAAAAAAAH!

The first to make a move was the dog, who

scuttled to the door and whined. Close on his heels came Boggy, pausing only to give the curtains a final tug as he sped out of the room.

"I thought the Germans had given it a miss," grumbled Ma, picking up bits of glass. "It'll probably go on all night as well, and we'll be too tired to eat the sausages I managed to get for breakfast. Come on all of you – into Mrs Moan's shelter."

"Never mind sausages – what about my perm?" Joanie wailed, as she pulled some folded blankets out of the sideboard. Drops of water dripped from her hair onto the floor.

"I don't think Hitler cares about your perm," said Heather, hauling pillows out of the corner cupboard.

Roy said nothing, but he picked up his gas mask and stuffed a book in his pocket.

Dad came back into the room, carrying two bottles of beer. "All ready?" he asked.

"All ready," the family chorused.

Hitler will send no Warning – so always carry your gas mask

Chapter 4
In the Shelter

It was snug in Mrs Moan's air-raid shelter.
Very snug. By the time Dad, Ma, Joanie,
Roy, Heather and the dog had piled in, there
wasn't much room for Mrs Moan and her fat
son, Hubert.

"It's *our* Anderson shelter," said Hubert
resentfully.* "The council gave us all one. Just
because you never put yours up –"

* *Find out about Anderson shelters on page 62*

"They didn't give us a *proper* shelter," Dad corrected. "They just dumped a load of corrugated iron outside the front door, and left us to put it up. Anyway, there's no space in our back garden."

"Thaarrs corrs izzfullar chyshins." Mrs Moan was having trouble speaking. She was having trouble because a cork was jammed between her teeth. Dad leant across and pulled it out.

"That's because it's full of chickens," she repeated.

"I don't remember you refusing any eggs." Dad tossed the cork in the air, caught it, then flicked it across the shelter. The cork missed Roy, but scored a direct hit on the dog's nose.

"If you don't keep your mouth open, the bomb blast bursts your ear-drums," said Mrs Moan, as she poked about under the dog. "You'll be sorry when you're deaf." She stuck the dirty cork back in her mouth.

"At least I'll have some peace. I think Gran's right to keep out of this hole."

Gran wouldn't go down the air-raid shelter. She'd taken one look at the puddles on the floor, and said that she'd rather die in the comfort of her own bed.

She had a point. During an air raid, sleep was impossible. The crack of guns and the whine and crash of bombs seemed to squeeze through the opening of the shelter and bounce round the corrugated iron sides.

Tonight's raid was even louder than usual.

"Where's Lenny?" asked Ma, shifting uncomfortably. She was sitting on top of the iron box which contained the family's ration books, her insurance policy, and Gran's will.

Joanie shook her damp hair. "He said he had to see a man about a dog."

Roy sniffed. "What's that awful smell?"

"It's gas!" cried Ma.

Mrs Moan spat out her cork. "Hubert, put your gas mask on!"

Hubert obeyed his mother. This made everyone feel more cheerful. Hubert had a fat

spotty face which looked much better when it was hidden by a gas mask.

"My Uncle Silas was gassed in the last war," volunteered Dad. "He survived, but he was never the same man. Lungs as raw as a piece of sliced liver."

Roy sniffed again. It was a horrible stink.

"It's Joanie's home-perm lotion," said Heather. "She's going to a dance with that Polish pilot tomorrow. He told her she looks like a film star."

"Why, you eavesdropping little –"

The whistle of a bomb cut off Joanie's

protests. A sudden gust of cold air blew round their feet as the shelter door flew open, and Lenny landed on his knees on the damp floor.

"Didn't you hear the siren?" asked Ma.

"I was on the lav," said Lenny, picking himself up, "keeping my bowels healthy, as instructed, and helping the War Effort."

"It'll need more help than that tonight." Dad cocked his head as the loudest bang of the evening made the walls of the shelter quiver. "That was a close one. Sounds as if Inkerman Road's copped it."

Hubert shook like a fat jelly and struggled to take off his gas mask. "My grandad says you can only be hit by a bomb if it's got your name on it."

"How do you know some German hasn't written Hubert Moon on a great big bomb?" Heather sounded pleased at the thought.

Hubert snivelled.

"Stop spreading alarm and despondency," said Mrs Moan. "They put people in prison for that, you know."

"And stop stuffing cotton wool in the dog's ears, Heather," said Ma.

"But Ma, the bombs make him nervous."

"It's a waste of resources."

"You can probably be put in prison for that, too," said Dad glumly.

"Give us a tune, Roy. Drown out the noise of those Germans."

Roy fished in his pocket for his mouth organ, shook it to get rid of any spit, and started to play. The dog threw back his head and howled dismally, but after a couple of bars everyone joined in the song and drowned his complaints.

"Run rabbit, run rabbit, run, run, run.
Don't give the farmer his fun, fun, fun.
He'll get by without his rabbit pie –"

Their caterwauling stopped abruptly, as the shelter shook to the noise of violent clattering. It sounded as if a tray of old tin cans had fallen on the roof.

At the same moment, the shelter door sprang open, and a grim face appeared at the entrance. It was Gran.

"Come on out! Lenny, Roy – all of you! They're dropping incendiary bombs! One's landed on our chicken shed!"

Chapter 5
To the Rescue

Roy was the first out of the shelter, and he chased after Gran as she darted through the hedge into their back garden. He'd never seen her move so fast. By the time he'd reached the hen house, she'd already put out one of the bombs with a bucket of sand.

Grabbing another bucket, Roy joined her. He'd had a lot of practice with incendiaries.

The fire bombs were dropped in clusters and, though they were only small, you had to get them out smartish.*

The garden was lit up like Bonfire Night. Hens were flapping and squawking all over the place.

"Quick," Gran shouted. "It'll stop them laying. We'll have no eggs for months."

Gran looked like a medieval knight in armour. Her shield was the lid of the pig-food bin, and her helmet was the metal vegetable strainer – secured with a scarf.

* *Find out about incendiary bombs on page 62*

She brandished a spade at Roy. "Here, use this! Cover the bombs with soil!"

Roy threw a pile of earth over a glowing incendiary. He missed, and accidently buried one of the chickens. Aiming more carefully, he tried again. The bomb fizzled and went out.

"Good shot! Get 'em out quick! If they start a fire it'll make an easy target for the next wave of bombers to aim at." Lenny was at his side, holding a sandbag in front of him to shield his eyes from the glare. "Cor, what a pong!"

"Yeah," shouted Dad, as he whacked an incendiary. "It's that mangy dog of Roy's. I don't know how it managed before the war, when there were no sandbags for it to wee on."

Roy smothered another fire bomb. "It's lucky Warden Marsh brought us some extra sandbags last night."

"Nothing to do with luck," bawled Dad. "That man's in league with Hitler. He always knows where the next packet's going to drop."

"Watch out! One's landed on Mrs Grubb's roof!"

Roy looked up. Lenny was right. One of the bombs had lodged in the gutter of the house next door, and was starting to blaze.

"Where's Ma Grubb?" yelled Lenny, trying to make himself heard above the squawks of the frightened chickens running round their feet.

"Staying with her sister, Gert," said Ma. "The house is empty."

"Yeah, that's why I stored the paint you gave me in their attic," said Roy.

"Oh my gawd." Lenny's jaw dropped. "You idiot. Paint's flammable. It'll go up like a bomb!"

Chapter 6
Manning the Pumps

The Pitts looked at each other in consternation.
The glare from the incendiaries lit their faces
with a ghostly light, and smelly fumes filled
the air.

"We'll all be burnt to death!" Mrs Moan
clutched Hubert.

"Where's our ladder?" shouted Dad,
looking round the garden.

"Don't ask," said Lenny. He narrowed his eyes and squinted at the fizzing bomb on the roof. "I'll see if I can reach it from here."

Snatching Roy's spade, he plunged it deep into the ground, and scooped up a mound of muddy earth. With a grunt, he hurled the spadeful of soil high in the air towards the gutter.

It fell short.

Most of the soil landed on Mrs Moan, who screamed loudly.

The soil that missed Mrs Moan landed on Hubert.

He screamed louder.

BANG! The garden gate sprang open and in strode Warden Marsh. "Now then. Now then. What's all this screaming about? Get yourselves organised."

Warden Boggy Marsh was carrying a stirrup pump,* which he put down on the ground with an impatient clank. Another warden, carrying two buckets, trotted in through the gate after him.

Boggy shoved Dad aside. "Stand back and let the trained men take charge." He surveyed the scene importantly. "This calls for a stirrup pump party. Bagshot!"

The second warden jumped and dropped his buckets, sloshing water on the ground. He was a very little man with large, thick glasses and an anxious expression.

* *Stirrup pumps were used to put out fires – see page 63*

"Now, get into line! Bagshot, you direct the pipe!" The little man grabbed hold of the hosepipe and waved the nozzle at the gutter.

"We need one person to pump," Boggy pushed Lenny over to the bucket, "and another to replenish the water." He nodded at Roy. "You, boy. Stand by. Now, on the count of three, commence pumping. One, two, three!"

The stirrup pump team performed as instructed. Roy hovered nearby, poised to grab

the bucket when it was empty. Lenny pushed the handle of the pump up and down vigorously, and Bagshot directed the hose.

A jet of water gushed into the air. It wasn't quite strong enough to reach the gutter, but it did a good job of soaking Mrs Moan and Hubert. The water fell on top of the soil that had already covered them.

Mrs Moan had stopped screaming. Her mouth opened and shut like a goldfish, but no sound came out. Hubert's face had turned a miserable shade of grey, and he grizzled quietly to himself.

"Pump harder, you useless chap," Boggy shouted. "The water's not reaching high enough." Lenny pumped harder, but the water still fell short, and the light from the bomb glowed even brighter. Small tongues of fire licked up the roof.

Dad shook his head. "This is hopeless." He pulled Heather and Roy aside. "How did you two get that paint up there in the first place?"

"There's a hole in our attic wall. We crawled through."

"Well you can just crawl back again and get that paint into our house. Look sharp!"

"Dad, they might be killed." Ma joined in the conversation. "That roof could go up like a torch any minute."

"All the more reason for them to get on with it," said Dad. "That paint'll fetch a lot of money. Get going, both of you. I'll keep these stupid wardens busy."

Roy looked round and saw that the action had moved on. A ladder had been found, but it wasn't long enough to reach the roof. Boggy was clinging to the top rung, and trying in vain

to poke at the bomb with a pole.

Dad wandered over to the foot of the ladder, whistling under his breath.

First he cast a casual glance to the left.

Then he shot an innocent look to the right.

Then he kicked the side of the ladder.

There was a loud scream.

"AAAAAAARGH!"

The ladder flew sideways and Boggy fell off it, sailing through the air like an acrobat. Luckily for him, he didn't land on the concrete path, but fell head first into the pig-food bin.

From the sound of his language, he didn't appreciate his good fortune.

"Get the paint and bring it round to the front of the house," Dad ordered, grabbing Roy by the shoulder. "I'll be there waiting to pick it up. Nobody'll notice, with this circus going on. *Get on with you*!"

Roy held back. The last thing he wanted to do was to return to the attic – the roof might burst into flames at any moment! But one look at Dad's face warned him that there was no point in arguing.

Heather had reached the same conclusion.

"We've got to do it," she said with a shrug. "Come on. I'm not scared."

"Who's scared?" Roy squared his shoulders and looked up at the flickering flames. "It's my mission," he announced firmly. "A daring raid. A race against time to save valuable paint from falling into enemy hands. Just obey my orders and follow me."

He turned to Heather, but there was no one there. She'd already gone back into the house!

IN THE BLACKOUT

Pause as you
leave the
stations light

Chapter 7
A Hot Spot

Heather had reached the top landing by the time Roy caught up with her. She'd dragged the chair into position and piled a couple of boxes on top of it. "Over to you," she said, turning to Roy.

He took a deep breath, scrambled up the unsteady tower, pushed open the trap door and wriggled through the gap. Heather watched his feet disappear into the black hole, and felt glad that it was Roy's mission, not hers.

It was dark in the loft. Dark and very hot. Jamming the trap door open with a piece of wood, Roy edged towards the far wall.

He squeezed through the hole into Mrs Grubb's house and returned as fast as he could, dragging the first tin of paint.

Then he stopped, and squatted back on his heels. Where was the open trap door? Why wasn't there any light?

Oh no! The piece of wood must have dislodged itself, and the trap door had fallen back into place. He groped for the crack, but he couldn't find it.

Gnawing worriedly at his thumb nail, he sat on the pot of paint and looked around him at the darkness. It felt even hotter – perhaps the bomb had already set the roof on fire? He couldn't get out! He was trapped in a stifling, air-less tomb . . .

"It's no good, men." Captain Roy Pitt looked around at the crew of his submarine. "I'm afraid that last torpedo did for us." His voice was steady. "We can't get back to the surface and there's only a few hours supply of air left. I'm sure you'll all behave like true Englishmen...

47

"Come on, I've been waiting for ages."
One edge of the trap door lifted up, and
Heather's voice floated through. Roy knelt on
the rafters and peered down. She'd managed to
poke open the trap door with a broom handle.

With a thankful sigh, he slid the
wooden square aside, and slowly
lowered the first pot of paint.
Heather stood on the chair and
grasped it carefully. "I bet it's
hot up there. You'd better be
quick. You might burn to death!"
"I can't go any faster. Take that
one to Dad, while I go back for the
other."

He watched Heather disappear
down the stairs, lugging the paint,
before he returned for the second tin.

Moving as quickly as he could, Roy
scrabbled over the heaped rubbish that littered
the floor. An old train set, a rocking horse,
Heather's play pen, a bit of rope –

Ah, that could come in useful, he thought.

Speedily returning with the second tin,
Roy tied the piece of old rope to the handle,
and lowered it to the floor. Then he clambered
down after it, wiped his hands on his shorts,
sat down on the tin and waited for Heather.

He waited. And waited. It was a long time
before she returned – still carrying the paint!

"Where've you been?" shouted Roy.

"Another load of incendiaries have landed
in the road at the front," Heather panted.
"Masses of people are trying to put them out.
Dad's surrounded by people. One of them's Mr
Harbottle – the man who owns the paint shop."
She looked at him meaningfully.

"Oh!" Roy thought for a minute. "Perhaps we'd better take the tins round to the back garden."

"We can't. I went there too – it's awful! Boggy's broken the kitchen window. Mrs Moan's having hysterics. That little warden's dropped a sandbag on one of Gran's chickens, and the dog's bitten Hubert."

"Good dog."

"Dad says we've got to hand the paint to

him out of the pantry window. It's the only one which isn't overlooked."

Picking up a tin each, they trooped into the pantry. Heather opened the small window as far as it would go. "Are you there, Dad?" she whispered.

"Get cracking!" Dad's angry voice floated from the outside. "Someone might come down the alley any minute."

"OK. First one coming now."

The window wasn't tall enough to allow the paint through upright. Turning the tin sideways, Roy carefully eased it out of the window. It was about halfway through when a familiar voice made him freeze.

"Mr Pitt! What do you think you're doing lurking here? We may have put out that bomb on the roof, but there's lots more of them round the front." It was Warden Marsh!

"And what's this sticking out of the window? We can't have rubbish obstructing the alley. Someone might bang into it and hurt themselves."

Straining his ears, Roy heard Dad mutter some excuse.

"Nonsense. It can't be stuck. All it needs is a short, sharp tug."

Roy felt the paint tin being wrenched from his grasp.

"AAAAAARGH!"

This long drawn-out yell was followed by a pause. Then a bubbling sigh.

Cautiously, Roy poked his head out of the small window. Below him in the alleyway, he could see two white statues!

One white statue wore a white tin helmet – the other wore a white cap.

As Roy looked down at them, a trickle of white paint dropped from the nose of the statue in the cap. It landed with a plop on the ground, next to the empty tin.

"What's happened?" whispered Heather, as she stuck her head out of the window. "Oh dear!" She went very quiet. "Do you think we'll get the blame?"

"Sure to."

"It wasn't *our* fault. We were only doing what we were told."

"It makes no difference." Roy's eyes met Heather's. "I think we'd better scarper."

"No point. They'll catch us in the end. They always do. Besides, it's sausages for breakfast."

"What'll we do?"

"Go and see if we can help. That way at least we look as if we're trying."

"I suppose you're right," said Roy glumly.

Leaving the remaining tin of paint on the pantry floor, they walked slowly out of the house and towards the alley.

Chapter 8
Joanie Takes Charge

Neither of the two white figures had moved. Shock appeared to have rooted them to the spot.

The statue wearing the tin hat was the first to find his voice. His mouth opened and a dribble of paint ran down his chin. "You're a disgrace. A German aircraft could spot you at ten thousand feet," he gurgled.

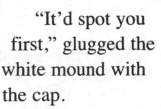

"It'd spot you first," glugged the white mound with the cap.

"Doesn't matter," said Lenny, joining Roy and Heather in their contemplation of the two statues. "You'll both be dead shortly from lead poisoning."

The remainder of the Pitt family straggled into the alley, and stared silently at the dripping white figures. The dog growled suspiciously.

Ma sniffed. "You smell dreadful! It reminds me of that lecture on poison gas we were given. You need decontaminating."

"They've taught us how to decontaminate people at my bandaging class," said Joanie, looking at the two white mounds with a gleam in her eye. "I've been looking for someone to practice on. First, you've got to scrub the contaminated person all over. I'll start running the bath. Come on."

Joanie grabbed Dad with one hand and
Warden Marsh with the other, and marched
them into the house. "You can look after the
others, Ma," she shouted over her shoulder.

Ma looked about her hopelessly.

Mrs Moan had collapsed on the ground.
Sitting next to her, blubbing, Hubert was
nursing his bitten knee. Bagshot was slumped
against the pig-swill bin, dazed. Gran had
walloped him so hard for killing her chicken
that he couldn't stand. At some point during
the evening's excitement, the cut on Lenny's
forehead had opened, and blood was streaming
down his face.

"I don't know where to start," said Ma faintly.

"Well, the dog's bandage has fallen off," said Roy.

Ma turned on him "It's all your fault."

"I was just doing what I was told. You *told* me to make sure that Dad was visible in the blackout. Well I have. He won't be having any more accidents." Roy smiled proudly.

"I suppose that's true," sighed Ma. She was a fair woman. Her eyes lifted towards the bathroom window.

"DON'T SCRUB SO HARD! I'LL HAVE NO SKIN LEFT!"

"AAAAARGH!"

"It sounds as if this decontamination business takes a long time," Ma said with a frown. "I'd better get on with the sausages." She brightened up at the thought.

"Bags I eat Dad's," said Heather.

NOTES

The Blackout

At the beginning of the Second World War, (1939 - 1945), the government ordered people not to let lights be seen at night. They wanted to prevent German pilots seeing where to drop their bombs.

The full blackout began on the night of 1st September 1939. Windows were covered with thick dark curtains, and some factory windows were painted black. All street lights were turned off, and cars crawled along the road without headlights. People were not allowed to use torches.

The first results of the blackout were alarming. That September, the number of road accidents doubled. In an attempt to make people safer, the goverment made changes to the rules. Cars were permitted to use headlamps, as long as they were masked, and

torches could be used, provided that the front was covered with layers of tissue paper.

The government suggested that everyone wore something white at night. Men kept their white shirt tails hanging out of their trousers when they went out at night, to make themselves more visible. Some farmers painted white stripes on their cows.

Anderson Shelters

Anderson shelters were named after Sir John Anderson, the minister responsible for civil defence. They were made from curved sheets of corrugated steel, bolted together at the top, and were erected in a hole in peoples' back gardens – like a kind of partly-sunken shed. Earth was then heaped on top of the roof.

The shelters were disliked because they were cramped (they were supposed to be able to sleep six adults), and flooded in wet weather. But they were very strong, and many families owed their lives to their shelter.

Bombs

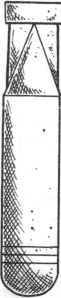

Several types of bombs were dropped by the Germans. The one kilo Electron incendiary bomb used by the Luftwaffe (German Air Force) was very effective. A heavy bomber could carry almost a thousand of these bombs. Their small size meant that they were easy to extinguish if dealt with right away, but, if left, they could start major fires.

Stirrup Pumps

The hand-operated stirrup pump was a useful tool for putting out fires caused by incendiary bombs. People kept buckets of water outside their homes in readiness. A team of three people manned the pumps. One pressed the pump up and down in the bucket of water, one directed the hose-pipe, and a third person stood by to fill up the bucket when all the water was used.

The government recommended that there should be seven stirrup pump teams to every thirty houses.

The Pitt Family

Gran

Dad

Joanie

Lenny

Ma

Heather

Roy

Find out more about how the Pitts survived the Second World War.

Digging for Victory 0 7496 6407 X

Spam! Whale meat! Boiled nettles! More Spam! The Pitts have had enough of food rationing. Then Lenny finds a crate of tinned fruit . . .

Careless Talk 0 7496 6406 1

A newcomer has arrived in Balaclava Terrace. He speaks with a foreign accent. He's got a small moustache. Is he a German spy? The Pitt family sets out to investigate.

Make Do and Mend 0 7496 6408 8

The Pitts are fed up with clothes rationing. They've nothing left to wear. Then Roy obtains a parachute, and the trouble begins . . .